Dilly Dally DAISY

Mark Fearing

DIAL BOOKS FOR YOUNG READERS an imprint of Penguin Group (USA) LLC

For Lily and Alyssa, who
taught me about dillydallying!

DIAL BOOKS FOR YOUNG READERS
Published by the Penguin Group
Penguin Group (USA) LLC
375 Hudson Street
New York, New York 10014

USA / Canada / UK / Ireland / Australia / New Zealand / India / South Africa / China
penguin.com
A Penguin Random House Company

Library of Congress Cataloging-in-Publication Data
Fearing, Mark, author, illustrator.
Dilly Dally Daisy / by Mark Fearing.
    pages cm
Summary: Daisy Marsha Martin's dilly dallying makes her late for nearly everything, but if she cannot find a way to
make it to her swimming lesson on time, her "mermaid training" will be at an end.
ISBN 978-0-8037-4065-5
[1. Tardiness—Fiction. 2. Humorous stories.] I. Title.
PZ7.F314Dil 2015   [E]—dc23   2014022149

Manufactured in China on acid-free paper

10 9 8 7 6 5 4 3 2 1

Designed by Jennifer Kelly
Text set in Hank BT

Daisy Marsha Martin is usually late.

She's late to breakfast because she's
teaching her stuffed animals gymnastics.

"Daisy! Your cereal is getting
soggy!" says Daisy's mom.

Daisy is late to piano lessons because she loves finding the low-low notes and singing along. Especially right before it's time to leave for piano lessons.

"I know we ask you to practice, but now is not the time, Daisy," says her mom.

Daisy is late to school because of just about everything.

I see the bus coming down the hill. Is your hair brushed?

"Ummm, just going to do that!" answers Daisy.

meow
meow
meow

Daisy thinks going up the stairs like a cat is way more fun. And faster. Maybe.

But where is Daisy's hairbrush?

Oh yeah.
That's not going to work.

So she decides to wear a hat instead.

But which one is the absolute best one?

The bus is headed down the street!

"On my way!" Daisy announces.

But her stuffies have to be able to see her get on the bus.

The bus that's pulling away from her house right now!

"Mom, you need to be the bus today.
Again," says Daisy.

On Saturday Daisy has swimming lessons, which she calls mermaid training. It's her favorite part of the entire week.

"Daisy, do you think you can be on time today?" asks her mom.

"I'll double, triple hurry, Mom!"
says Daisy. She races up the stairs,
not even pretending to be a cat.

But her favorite bathing suit is busy.

Putting that suit on means Penny Penguin is going to be cold.
That means Daisy isn't the only one who needs a towel.
So Daisy goes to the laundry room.

After a few tries, she gets what she needs.

"I'm ready! Sort of—almost!" says Daisy.

She puts on her
favorite shorts,

which is always more
fun when you dance.

All she needs now is
her mermaid shirt.

But it's in the
hamper—dirty!

Daisy can't go to
mermaid lessons
without that shirt!

Everything is ruined.
No mermaid shirt means no
mermaid lessons today or ever!

Daisy was so close to being ready.

Maybe, just maybe, she can go to mermaid lessons without that shirt? After all, who else will teach her stuffies about pool safety?

She's the only mermaid in the house.

Daisy knows what she must do.

"I will not be late! I can do this," she declares.

Daisy picks out a different shirt.

But the shirt she
grabs is too small!

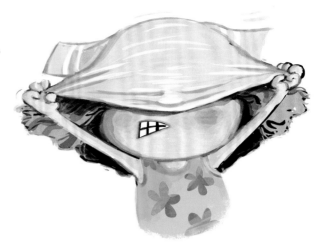

She tries holding her breath,
hoping it will make her head
smaller. It doesn't help.

She yanks the shirt with
everything she has!

There is no time to search
the mess for a clean shirt
so Daisy grabs her mermaid
shirt—from the hamper.

You can hardly see the
mud on it. Or the mustard.
Or the . . . whatever it is.

Then flip-flops and
her backpack.

She picks a hat, the towel,
and takes off!

Daisy runs downstairs faster than Christmas morning.
She never knew being on time could be so much fun.

Daisy Marsha Martin looks like a bright
summer's day in the middle of December.

"At least put a coat on," says Daisy's mom.

But which coat would be exactly right
wonders Daisy Marsha Martin.